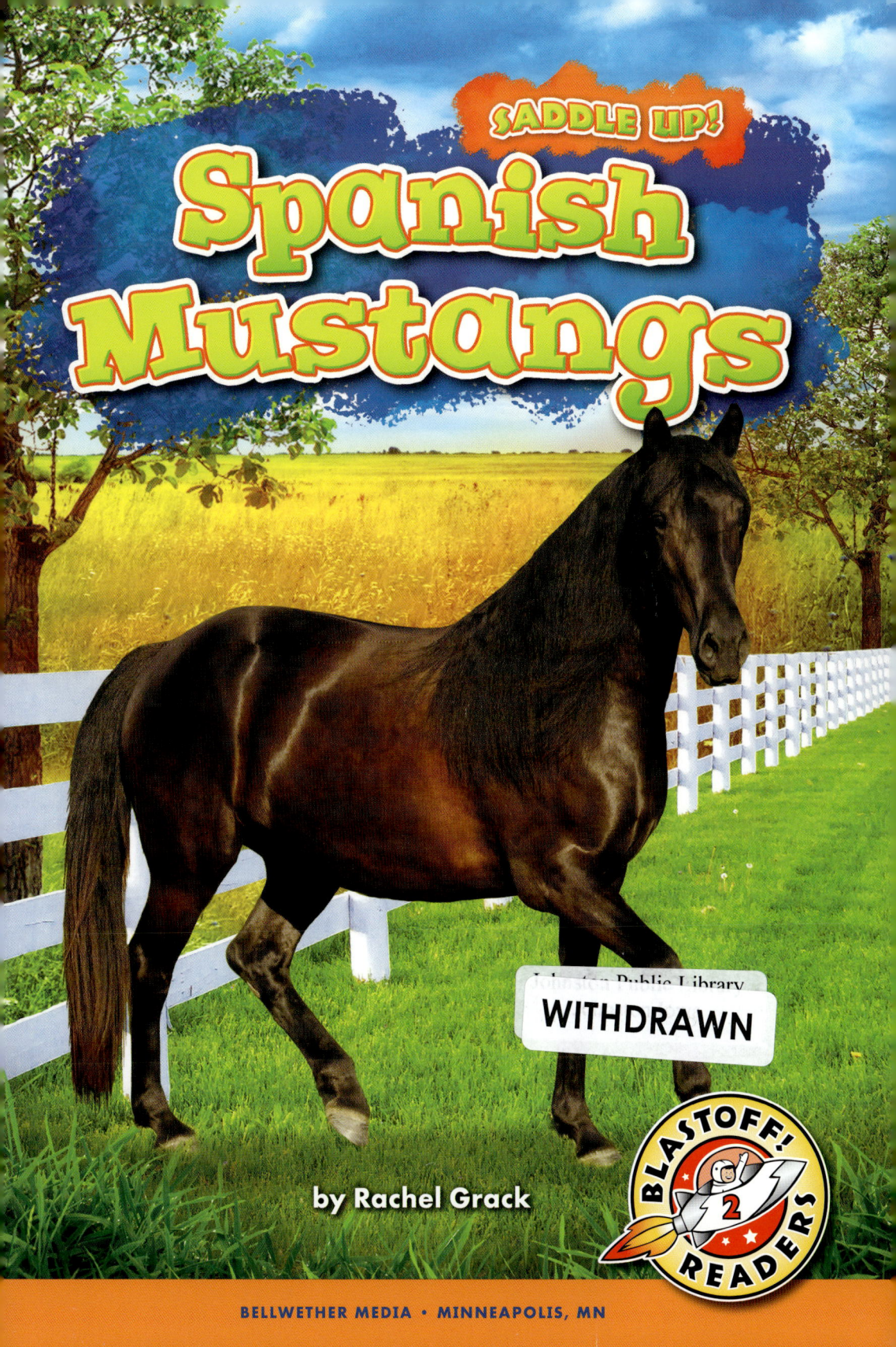

SADDLE UP!
Spanish Mustangs

by Rachel Grack

BELLWETHER MEDIA • MINNEAPOLIS, MN

BLASTOFF! READERS 2

Blastoff! Readers are carefully developed by literacy experts to build reading stamina and move students toward fluency by combining standards-based content with developmentally appropriate text.

Level 1 provides the most support through repetition of high-frequency words, light text, predictable sentence patterns, and strong visual support.

Level 2 offers early readers a bit more challenge through varied sentences, increased text load, and text-supportive special features.

Level 3 advances early-fluent readers toward fluency through increased text load, less reliance on photos, advancing concepts, longer sentences, and more complex special features.

★ **Blastoff! Universe**

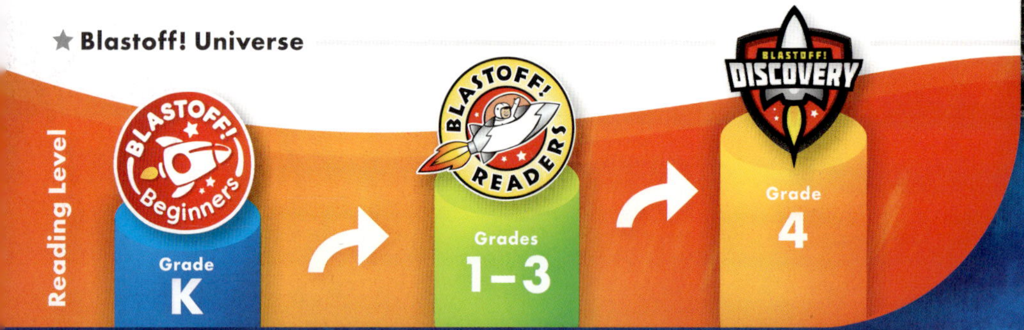

Grade K

Grades 1-3

Grade 4

Reading Level

This edition first published in 2021 by Bellwether Media, Inc.

No part of this publication may be reproduced in whole or in part without written permission of the publisher. For information regarding permission, write to Bellwether Media, Inc., Attention: Permissions Department, 6012 Blue Circle Drive, Minnetonka, MN 55343.

Library of Congress Cataloging-in-Publication Data

Names: Koestler-Grack, Rachel A., 1973- author.
Title: Spanish mustangs / by Rachel Grack.
Description: Minneapolis, MN : Bellwether Media, Inc., 2021. | Series: Saddle up! | Includes bibliographical references and index. | Audience: Ages 5-8 | Audience: Grades K-1 | Summary: "Relevant images match informative text in this introduction to Spanish mustangs. Intended for students in kindergarten through third grade"– Provided by publisher.
Identifiers: LCCN 2020033247 (print) | LCCN 2020033248 (ebook) | ISBN 9781644874325 (library binding) | ISBN 9781648341090 (ebook)
Subjects: LCSH: Mustang–Juvenile literature.
Classification: LCC SF293.M9 K64 2021 (print) | LCC SF293.M9 (ebook) | DDC 636.1/3–dc23
LC record available at https://lccn.loc.gov/2020033247
LC ebook record available at https://lccn.loc.gov/2020033248

Text copyright © 2021 by Bellwether Media, Inc. BLASTOFF! READERS and associated logos are trademarks and/or registered trademarks of Bellwether Media, Inc.

Editor: Elizabeth Neuenfeldt   Designer: Laura Sowers

Printed in the United States of America, North Mankato, MN.

Table of Contents

Sturdy Horses	4
Powerful Beauties	6
Spanish Mustang Beginnings	12
Tireless Friends	18
Glossary	22
To Learn More	23
Index	24

Sturdy Horses

Spanish mustangs are smart and **sturdy** horses. Many can **thrive** in the wild.

These strong horses never give up in tough times!

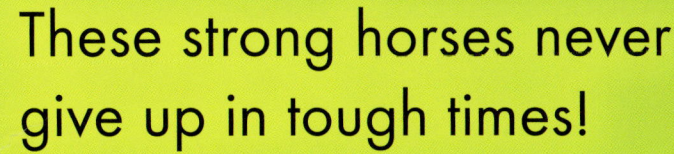

Powerful Beauties

Spanish mustangs look smooth and **muscular**. They have short backs, deep chests, and low-set tails.

Most stand between 13 and 15 **hands** high.

Size of a Spanish Mustang

one hand = 4 inches (10 centimeters)

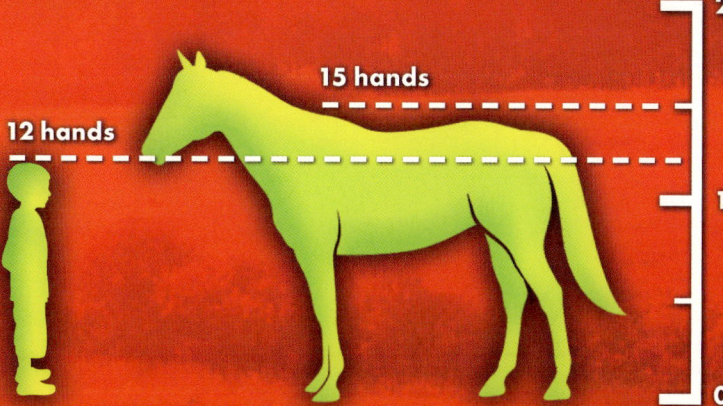

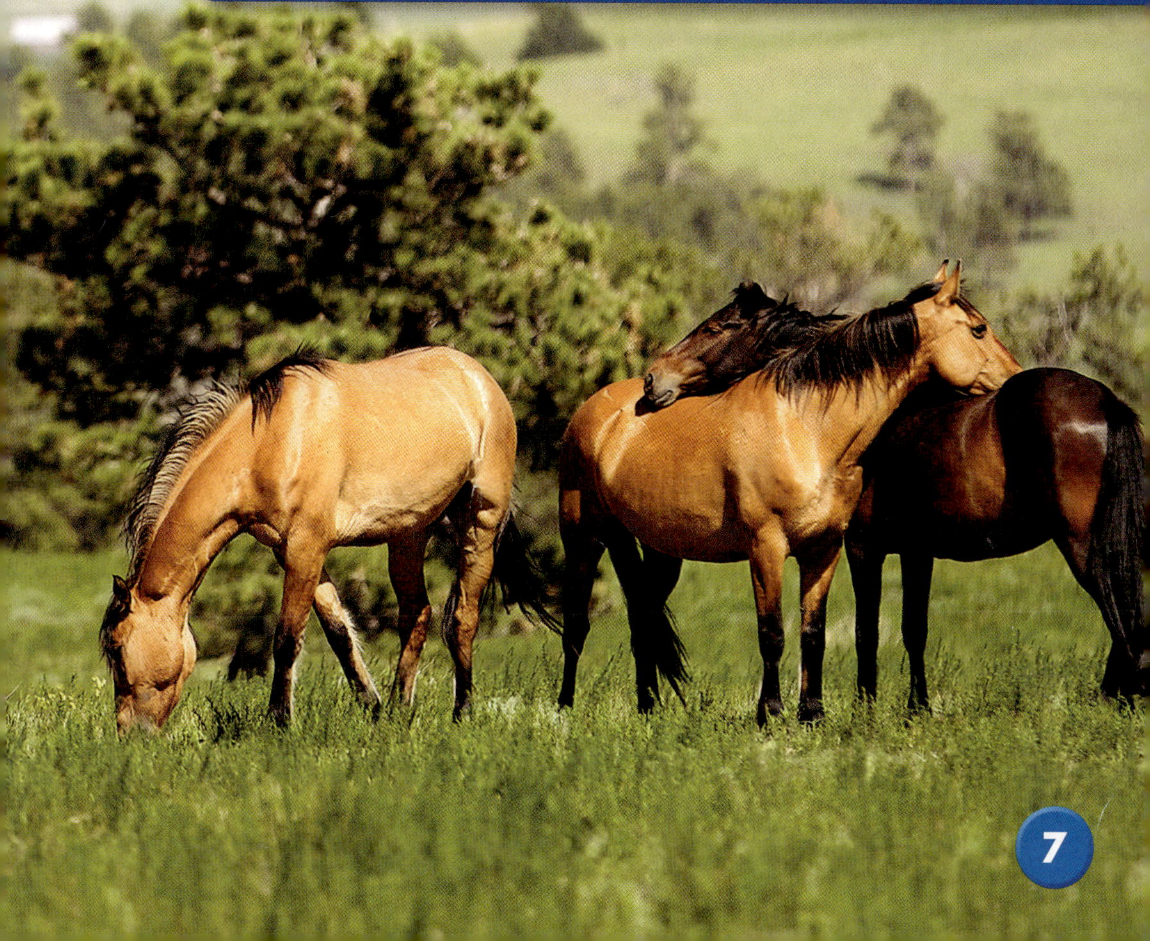

Spanish mustangs have powerful legs. They have hard, thick **hooves**.

hooves

These help the mustangs walk on rocky and uneven ground.

Spanish mustangs come in many beautiful colors. Their **coats** are shades of brown, black, and white.

They can have spots and stripes, too!

Coat Colors

brown

black

white

Spanish Mustang Beginnings

Comanche horsemen

Spanish mustangs started in Spain. Around 1500, **explorers** brought them to the Americas.

Native Americans were skilled **horsemen**. They quickly began using these horses. They helped the **breed** grow!

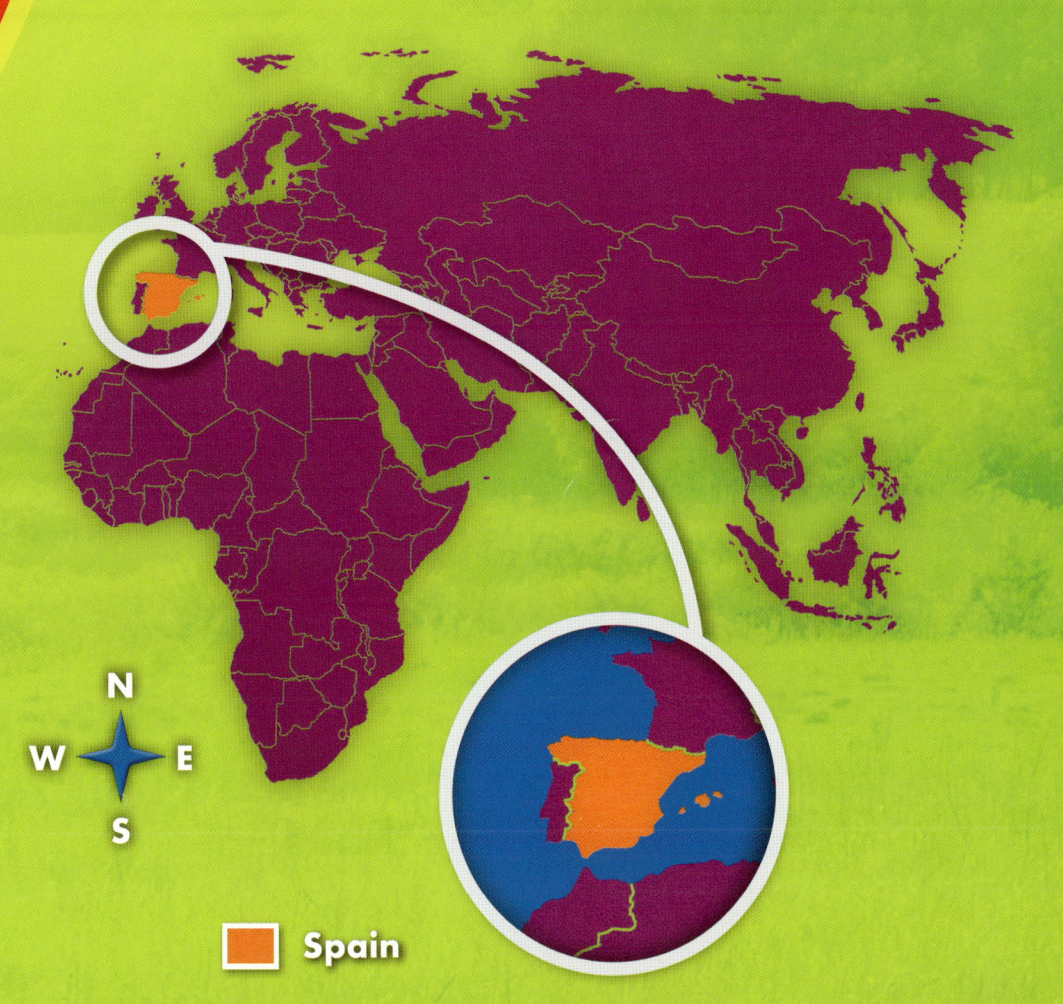

Spain

As time passed, some mustangs escaped or ran away.

By the 1800s, thousands of Spanish mustangs ran wild!

Between 1890 and the 1950s, some people did not want Spanish mustangs around. The breed almost went **extinct**.

Spanish Mustang Timeline

Around 1500
Spanish explorers bring Spanish mustangs to the Americas

1800s
Thousands of Spanish mustangs live in the wild

1890
Many mustangs begin to die

1957
The Spanish Mustang Registry forms

In 1957, the Spanish Mustang Registry formed. It helped save the breed!

Tireless Friends

Spanish mustangs are always ready to work. They have great **endurance**. Farmers use them for **herding** cows.

Mustangs also wow **rodeo** crowds in roping events!

Horsing Around
Rodeo Gear Checklist

✓ **cowboy hat or helmet**

✓ **gloves**

✓ **saddle**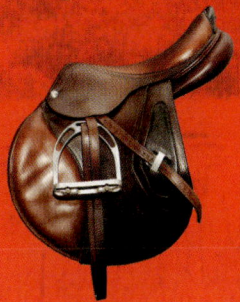

✓ **rope**

Spanish mustangs like to please their owners. They quickly become true friends.

These loving horses will happily carry riders the extra mile!

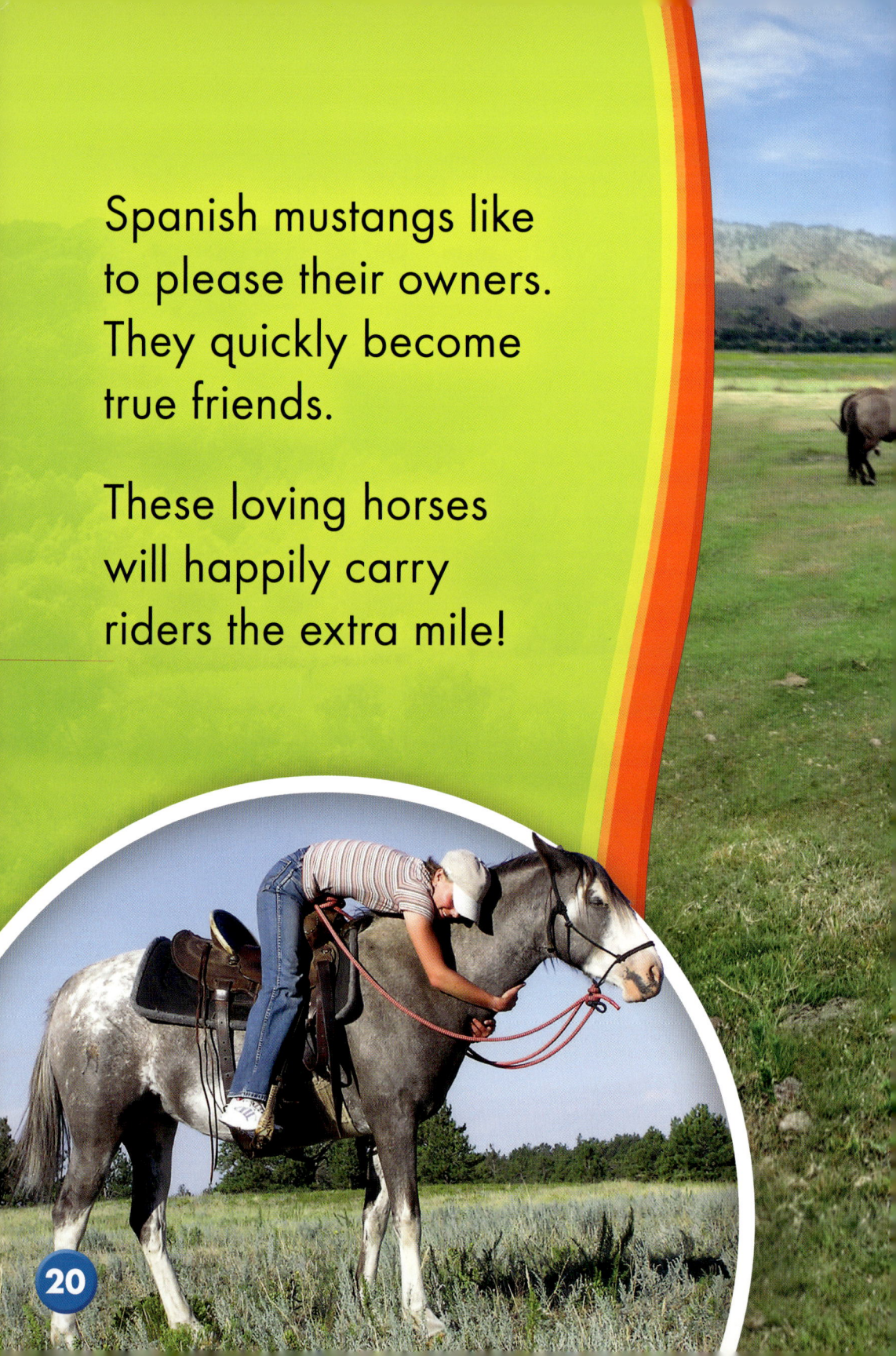

Glossary

breed—a certain type of horse

coats—the hair or fur covering some animals

endurance—the ability to keep going for a long time

explorers—people who travel in search of information

extinct—to have completely died out

hands—the units used to measure the height of a horse; one hand is equal to 4 inches (10 centimeters).

herding—controlling the movements of animals

hooves—the hard coverings on the feet of animals such as horses and pigs

horsemen—people who are skilled in riding and raising horses

muscular—related to strong and large muscles; muscles help animals and humans move.

rodeo—a show in which riders perform certain skills on horses

sturdy—strong and well built

thrive—to do very well

To Learn More

AT THE LIBRARY

Dell, Pamela. *Mustangs*. New York, N.Y.: AV2 by Weigl, 2019.

Grack, Rachel. *American Paint Horses*. Minneapolis, Minn.: Bellwether Media, 2021.

Hansen, Grace. *Mustang Horses*. Minneapolis, Minn.: Abdo Kids Jumbo, 2020.

ON THE WEB

FACTSURFER

Factsurfer.com gives you a safe, fun way to find more information.

1. Go to www.factsurfer.com.
2. Enter "Spanish mustangs" into the search box and click 🔍.
3. Select your book cover to see a list of related content.

Index

Americas, 12
backs, 6
breed, 13, 16, 17
chests, 6
coats, 10, 11
colors, 10, 11
endurance, 18
explorers, 12
extinct, 16
farmers, 18
herding, 18
hooves, 8
horsemen, 12, 13
legs, 8
Native Americans, 13
riders, 20
rodeo, 19
roping, 19

size, 6, 7
Spain, 12, 13
Spanish Mustang Registry, 17
spots, 11
stripes, 11
tails, 6
timeline, 17
wild, 4, 15
work, 18

The images in this book are reproduced through the courtesy of: Juniors Bildarchiv GmbH/ Alamy, cover; karenparker2000, pp. 4-5, 11 (black), 16-17; Mark J. Barrett/ Alamy, pp. 5, 14-15; Rita Robinson, pp. 6, 10-11, 18-19; Jennifer Stone, pp. 6-7; Jim Snyders/ Alamy, p. 8; John_Wijsman, pp. 8-9; BHamms, p. 11 (brown); Winthrop Brookhouse, pp. 11 (white), 20; Hirarchivum Press/ Alamy, pp. 12-13; simpleman, p. 19 (cowboy hat); worldinmyeyes.pl, p. 19 (gloves); Alexey Wraith, p. 19 (saddle); SHTRAUS DMYTRO, p. 19 (rope); A L Christensen/ Getty Images, pp. 20-21.